W9-AKY-093

E
Bra

Braun, Lutz

Faster than the bull

DATE DUE

Faster Than the Bull

Story by Lutz Braun

Illustrations by Stephen Moore

RSVP

RAINTREE
STECK-VAUGHN
P U B L I S H E R S
The Steck-Vaughn Company

Austin, Texas

I dedicate this book to my grandmother in England;
To my parents for their understanding, care, and love;
To my brother and sisters;
To Miss Sullivan for her belief in me;
and to all the runners of the "Running of the Bulls." — **L.B.**

To Laura with love. — **S.M.**

1 2 3 4 5 6 7 8 9 0   RRD   97 96 95 94 93 92

Library of Congress Number: 92–37947

Library of Congress Cataloging-in-Publication Data

Braun, Lutz, 1980–
   Faster than the bull / story by Lutz Braun; illustrations by Stephen Moore.
       p.   cm. — (Publish-a-book)
   Summary: A thirteen-year-old boy from a small village in the mountains of Spain pursues his dream of winning the dangerous Running of the Bulls race.
   1. Children's writings, American.   [1. Running the bulls — Fiction. 2. Spain — Fiction. 3. Children's writings.]   I. Moore, Steve, 1956– ill.   II. Title.   III. Series.
PZ7.B73776Fas   1993   [Fic] — dc20   92–37947
                                                                                 CIP
ISBN 0–8114–3580–6   AC

Up on the high peaks of the mountains in Spain lay a small village. 'Twas the late hour of eight o'clock when Gonzalo Sánchez was born. He began working at the tender age of five on his father's farm. Every day Gonzalo had to run a couple of miles uphill to catch the goats before supper. This made his legs strong and muscular.

On his thirteenth birthday, Gonzalo made a wish to conquer his destiny — winning the Running of the Bulls. This tradition was a very popular but dangerous event in Spain. For it is said, "If the bull is faster than thee, luck or death shall meet thee." Gonzalo was assured by his parents that he could participate in the race.

That afternoon when the sun was going down, the sky was filled with a dark brilliance of red and orange. Gonzalo sat on the hillside and thought about his plans for the race. His uncle had entered the Running of the Bulls, but he had never returned. This made Gonzalo uneasy. The thought of his uncle's fate would stay with him throughout the race. But he vowed to do what his uncle had not.

He would have to start early on his adventurous journey to the great city. He would have to travel across the harsh mountains, then along a shining river, and finally walk fifty tiring miles.

When the morning came, Gonzalo was ready. He kissed and hugged his family good-bye, for when and if he returned, he would be a noble adult.

He set off into the distance with a stout heart and a determined mind. He climbed across the rugged mountains and walked the strenuous miles to the river.

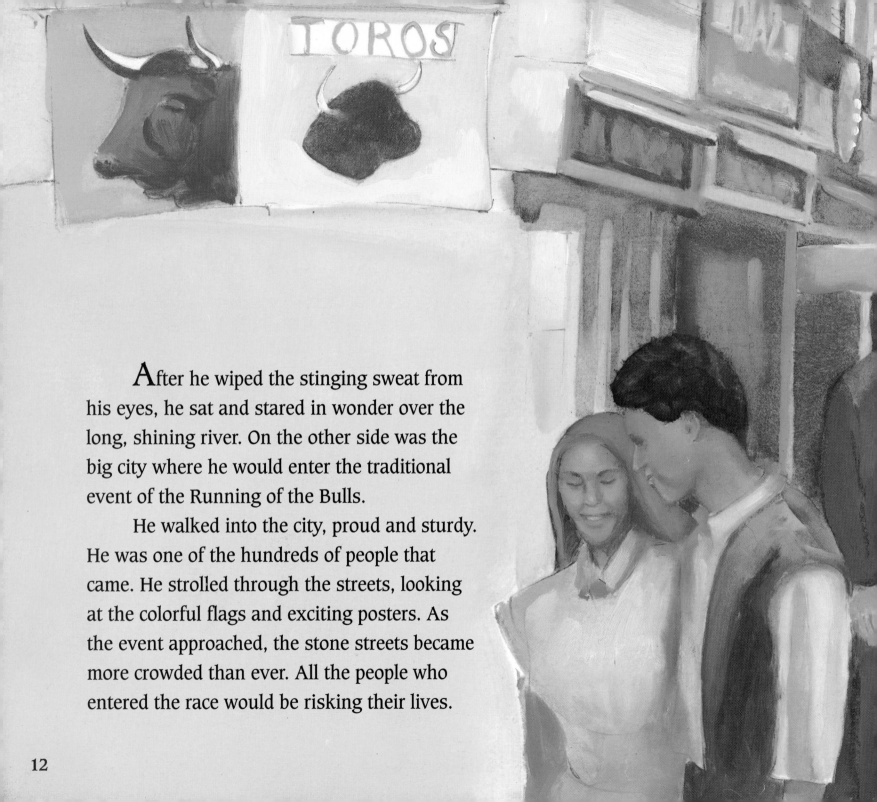

After he wiped the stinging sweat from his eyes, he sat and stared in wonder over the long, shining river. On the other side was the big city where he would enter the traditional event of the Running of the Bulls.

He walked into the city, proud and sturdy. He was one of the hundreds of people that came. He strolled through the streets, looking at the colorful flags and exciting posters. As the event approached, the stone streets became more crowded than ever. All the people who entered the race would be risking their lives.

13

Gonzalo went to his room at the old inn and fell on the bed. He had walked and climbed over one hundred exhausting miles to get here. The only light in his room was a torch of fire. He stared at the gleaming flame as he thought of his home, his family, and then, the race. He yawned softly and slowly fell asleep.

The next morning he walked to the field where the bulls were kept. He studied the bulls until he came to the strongest-looking one.

An old man who was passing by told Gonzalo that last year a terrible disaster had happened because the bull had either shoved the runners out of the way or disposed of them. This made Gonzalo shiver. Then he thought of his beloved uncle who once had a dream that ended his life. He asked the old man why they didn't kill the bull after the race was over.

The man looked up with sparkling eyes and a wrinkled face and said, "They do not slay the bull unless someone has defeated it. Last year a man named Gastón Sánchez almost won, but he was speared from behind by the terrible bull."

The bull looked at Gonzalo with its red, shining eyes as if it knew him. Tears formed in Gonzalo's eyes -– tears that would help him win the race.

Gonzalo walked back toward the streets as darkness approached and silence filled the great city. In two more days the race would begin.

He went to his room and lit the torch. Many runners who cherish their families write a note of love and hope to them before the race, for anything could happen. Gonzalo picked up his pen.

The two days passed quickly, and the streets were suddenly empty. People crowded at their windows, on their roofs, and in their doorways. Anyone out on the streets at this time could be crushed.

There would be five bulls in the race, including the one Gonzalo had seen a few days ago. The bulls looked even more fierce than they had then.

A man from the tower signaled for the race to begin.
All the runners started to shove each other to get ahead.
Gonzalo was slowed by the other men. He finally pushed
his way through and took off at a fast pace. The bulls were
let go. They put on speed, eliminating the runners in their
way. Gonzalo did not look back, for it would slow him
down. The nimble runner sped through the city. The
crowds were cheering loudly. Gonzalo had a good lead
over the bulls, but one bull was catching up.

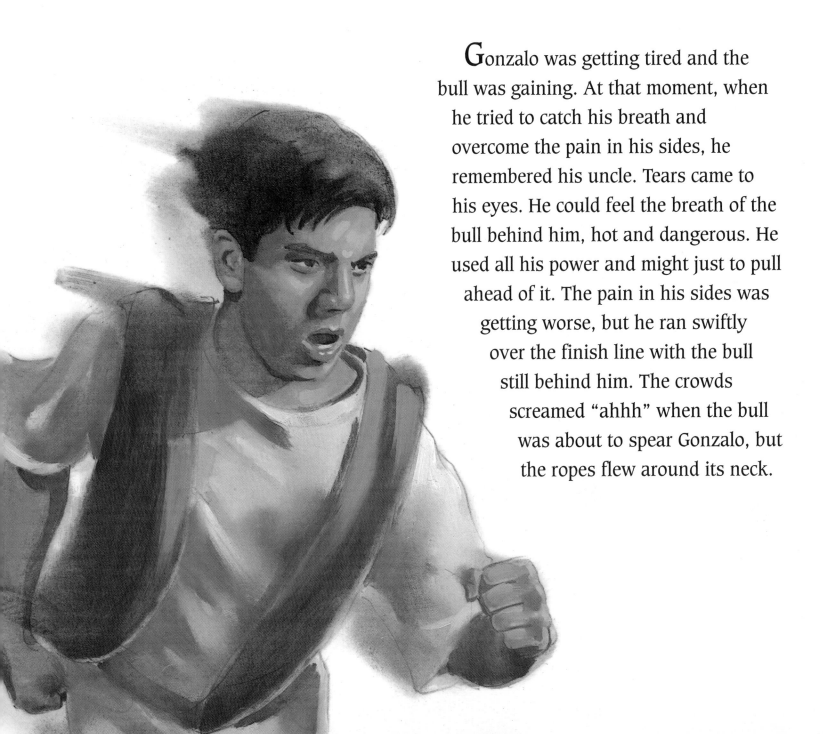

Gonzalo was getting tired and the bull was gaining. At that moment, when he tried to catch his breath and overcome the pain in his sides, he remembered his uncle. Tears came to his eyes. He could feel the breath of the bull behind him, hot and dangerous. He used all his power and might just to pull ahead of it. The pain in his sides was getting worse, but he ran swiftly over the finish line with the bull still behind him. The crowds screamed "ahhh" when the bull was about to spear Gonzalo, but the ropes flew around its neck.

Gonzalo fell to the ground in great pain. The crowd roared louder than ever. A few men came over to Gonzalo and carried him on their shoulders. His throat was dry and the sweat stung his eyes. A woman wiped his noble face. There was going to be a big fiesta because they had a winner of the Running of the Bulls.

After a few weeks, Gonzalo Sánchez
returned home. His parents praised him
highly, for he had done what he had vowed.
Gonzalo sat outside as the sun went down,
looked over the valleys and streams, and
simply smiled.

Lutz Braun, the author of **Faster Than the Bull**, was born in San Dimas, California, in 1980 and now lives in La Habra Heights, California. He has one older brother, Sigmar, and two older sisters, Tanya and Natalia. Natalia is also a writer and inspired Lutz with her creative writing. Lutz's father, Helmut, works as an industrial chemist, and Lutz considers his mother, Sandra, a great mom and housewife.

Lutz likes writing and reading books that have adventure. He feels that writing books will always stay a hobby of his. He also enjoys playing many sports, especially football and basketball.

Lutz attends Our Lady of Guadalupe Catholic School in La Habra, California. The school librarian, Kathy Garcia, sponsored him in this Publish-a-Book Contest. One of his sixth grade teachers, Miss Sullivan, inspired him by teaching him to imagine that he was the character in the story, and to feel, hear, and smell what that character would. After high school, Lutz wants to go to college and get a degree, perhaps in archaeology. He knows that he will keep on writing. He says, "To me, writing a story is putting a dream on paper!"

The twenty honorable-mention winners in the **1992 Raintree/Steck-Vaughn Publish-a-Book Contest** were Heidi Roberts of Dresden, Maine; Jessica McCulla of Mesa, Arizona; Kristine Laughlin of Mount Laurel, New Jersey; Tori Miner of Franklin, Connecticut; Brittany Kok of Decatur, Illinois; Hilary Manske of Clintonville, Wisconsin; Mandy Baldwin of Bothell, Washington; Kristin Yoshimoto of Honolulu, Hawaii; Arwen Miller of Kent, Ohio; Jessica Martin of Wauwatosa, Wisconsin; Jessa Queyrouze of Mandeville, Louisiana; Kay-Lynn Walters of Fostoria, Ohio; Karen Lauffer of Edgewater, Maryland; Karey Vaughn of Somerset, Pennsylvania; Matthew Kuzio of Mandeville, Louisiana; Leonard Ford of Germantown, Tennessee; Carolyn Hack of Overland Park, Kansas; Emily Levasseur of Hudson, New Hampshire; Christina Miller of Port Jefferson, New York; and Shawna Smith of Hays, Kansas.

Stephen Moore is a native of Utah and graduate of Utah State. He enjoys politics as a spectator sport and ice cream. He revels in living in New York City with his wife, Laura.

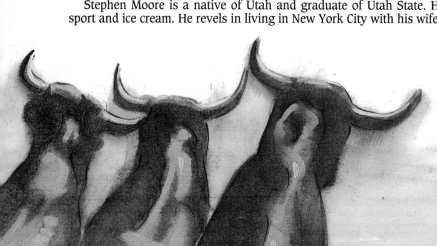